This Walker book belongs to:

_____

_____

_____

For my friends Cliff and Carisa!

First published 2017 by Walker Books Ltd
87 Vauxhall Walk, London SE11 5HJ

This edition published 2018

2 4 6 8 10 9 7 5 3 1

This book has been typeset in Myriad

Printed in China

British Library Cataloguing in Publication Data:
a catalogue record for this book is available from the British Library

ISBN 978-1-4063-7980-8

www.walker.co.uk

BOO WHO?

BEN CLANTON

WALKER BOOKS

AND SUBSIDIARIES

LONDON • BOSTON • SYDNEY • AUCKLAND

This is Boo.

Boo is new.

Being new can be scary,
even when everyone is friendly.

Boo has trouble fitting in.

He can't play bounce-ball.

Or pick-up twigs.

Or tag.

Would anyone even care
if Boo just disappeared?

BOO-HOO

**Everyone else has started
a game of hide-and-seek.**

Soon Gizmo finds Rex.

And Wild.

And Sprinkles.

But where is Boo?

Everyone helps look.

At last, a game that Boo can play!

This is Boo.
He's new, but he fits right in.